# Shadow
# the Cat Detective

# ...and other stories

A Read Aloud Story For Children and their Adults

**By**

Written By

## John Stewart Langley

Reading some stories together
making it up as we go
speaking in make-believe voices
going along with the flow

Taking a little time out of our day
away from the chaos and fuss
avoiding any distractions
these moment's are only for us

For tomorrow we might not remember
though how could we ever forget
these times that we have together
here we go... one, two, ready, get set...

ISBN: 1838017743
ISBN-13: 978-1-8380177-4-3

To Our Three Sons
Robert, Iain and Michael,
their soul-mates
Sophie, Laura and Kirst
and our fabulous grandkids
Abbie, Benjamin and James


May you never completely grow up.


With Thanks for just being you

# Shadow

# the Cat

# Who is Shadow?

She can disappear in darkness
just by closing up her eyes
She can slink about the house
without making any noise
And when you try to find her
she'll have hidden out the way
cos she's Shadow the Detective
and she likes to save the day

She listens to your stories
and tries to help a lot
when you're mind is in a tizz-wazz
and you've almost lost the plot
she'll consider all the angles
in every kind of way
cos she's Shadow the Detective
and she always saves the day

She'll prowl around and scratch her head
just like a real detective
she'll lift her tail and turn three times
which always is effective
then she'll pounce upon the very clue
that everyone has missed
cos she's Shadow the Detective
- have I given you the gist?

She's such a special cat she is
all black with yellow eyes
and if and when you meet her
she might give you a surprise
and help you solve a problem
that was ruining your day
cos she's Shadow the Detective
and she likes to have her say

Yes, she's Shadow the Detective
and very black, not grey
yes, she's Shadow the Detective
who sometimes likes to play
and when she goes and spots the clues
which is clever for a cat
she's likely to just save the day
cos she's very good at that !

# Where is she?

Who's that lying in the corner
who's that climbing up the walls
who's that looking at me from that tree
ignoring all my calls?

Can you see her? I hope she knows how to get down...

She can vanish in the shadows
she can land on all four feet
you can see that she's a marvel
when you meet her on the street

Can you see her ?

She's hiding in the shadows

If you would like to meet her
when she's curled up in her room
then don't make a noise, just tiptoe
and peer into the gloom
then if you're lucky you'll spot her
a Shadow in the black
just a glimpse, be quick or you'll miss her
because she's got the knack
of disappearing so quickly
you'll wonder 'Was that her?'
was that movement really Shadow
lying on that chair
was that her eye a-winking
from the middle of the dark
or has she gone already
and is half way to the park.

# Shadow's Main Claim to Fame

If you really need to find a thing
that unfortunately you've lost
a ring, a phone, a precious jewel
or something that only cost
a bit less...

...like a button, or a sock
or a chewed up shoe

and you've hunted and you've hunted
and you still don't have a clue...

...then that's the time for you to meet
this clever friend of mine
a really smart detective
and even more than that
a slinky, intelligent feline,
a super special black cat.

Her name is not Sherlock, nor Vera
nor Marple nor Clarice nor Hera
but Shadow the cat
a Detective at that
and she likes to sit on her mat

Here she is on her favourite mat, she sleeps on it a lot.

It's warm and cosy and right by the fire.

Now there's many a story
I could tell you
about Shadow and clues
and all that
so I've chosen a one
I remember quite well
a mystery that I couldn't solve

I think  I can tell it
from beginning to end
so we'd better get started,
let's see what happened...

Shadow is getting ready for
the story by licking her paws...
Are you ready?

# The Short Tale of Shadow and the Lost Gold Ring

I looked out the kitchen window
while finishing off my chores
I wished I was outside right now
and not cooped up here indoors

I was just finishing some washing up
Shadow was watching me from her mat

I wanted to go for a walk you see
so I rushed to finish the dishes
then threw on my coat, pulled on my boots
and went to follow my wishes

When I got outside I sighed with relief
and headed off down the lane
I'd left Shadow asleep on her mat you see
but I would soon see her again

Can you see her asleep on the mat?
its quite difficult isn't it...

....she seems almost to disappear
- you have to  look carefully...

I'd only gone for a little walk
it wasn't very far
I'd taken a flask of tea with me
but I didn't need the car

I soon sat down upon a branch
with mushrooms growing near

I poured myself a cup of tea

and then I saw a deer!

Can you see the deer?

I kept as still as still could be
I didn't want to scare it
I was so pleased to see it there
I nearly couldn't bear it

It had just sneaked out of the trees
one of nature's pride and joy
even though I couldn't tell from here
if it was a girl or a boy

My excitement it was so intense
I spilt a bit of tea
the liquid it was still quite hot
as it splashed onto my knee

...and then it fell on to the ground
and though I tried to make no sound
I twitched and squirmed
and rubbed my knee...

and the deer it soon raised its head...

and twitched its ears...

and turned my way...

and looked at me

and I knew I had been spotted!

When the deer saw me it ran away
flashing it's white bum

See

I screwed the top back on my flask
and went back the way I'd come

I'd only walked a step or two
when I saw something was wrong
the fingers on my hand were bare
... my golden ring was gone!

Look! - There's no ring
on any of these fingers!!

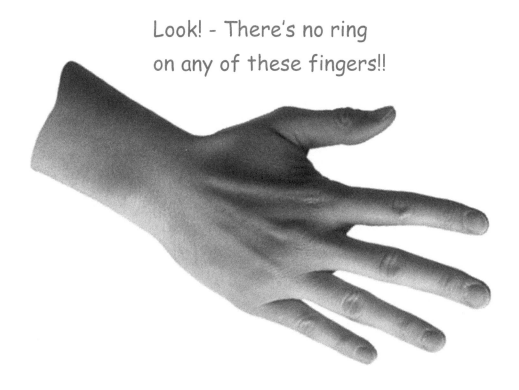

I went straight back to where I'd sat
and desperately looked around
I scraped and searched and hunted
but nothing could be found

I asked an Owl who said 'To-whoo,
there's really nothing I can do.'

Can you see the Owl?

I asked some lambs who said 'Oh dear!'
as they stood under a tree
and although they were very sorry
they were sure they couldn't help me

Here are the lambs.
They are with their
Mummy.

I even asked a Robin
who was hopping to and fro
but he couldn't help me either
and he said he had to go

So I hurried home to ask for help
I knew just who to talk to
I needed someone very clever
and I thought I knew just who

Cos when there's something that you've lost
that you really cannot find
there's someone clever that I know
who is helpful and quite kind

Do you know just who I mean?
Someone who's lying on her mat
of course you do it's our old friend
the amazing... Shadow Cat!

She's starting to
wake up – maybe
she senses there's
a problem

So when I got home I shouted out
"Oh Shadow Cat! I need your help
I know that you can help me out
just as you've done before."

Here she is
waking up
even more
... with a big
yaaaawn...

Then while she listened
I told her the tale
I told it quite slowly
in every detail

I said that I'd looked
for the ring that I'd lost
a thing that's worth more
than it actually cost

how I'd hunted and hunted
and still had no clue
and now couldn't think
of what more I could do

I looked in the corner
where she sat on her mat
she was shaking her head
looking this way and that

and then she got up
on her shiny black feet
climbed off of her mat
and looking quite neat

she sauntered towards me

with her bright yellow eyes
and looked up upon me
with a look of surprise

See her look of
surprise?

Oh Shadow Cat, Oh Shadow Cat
please help me find this thing
Oh Shadow Cat, Oh Shadow Cat
help find my precious ring

She slo-o-owly stretched

then moved towards my feet
she sidled and she slunk

then jumped up on a seat

She's not normally allowed to jump on here...

She seemed to be asking
what I thought I had done
and looked like she thought
that this might be fun

"Oh Shadow Cat, Oh Shadow Cat
this is really not meant
to be fun
Oh Shadow Cat, Oh Shadow Cat
please find out
what I've gone and done."

"I had it this morning
on this finger here
it can't have gone far
it must be quite near

but I cannot find it
I've looked everywhere
I know its outside
but I don't know quite where."

She looked at me sternly
with her round yellow eyes
and seemed to be saying
she'd give it a try

She's making the
most of being up
there...

But she didn't go out
as I thought that she would
instead she inspected the kitchen
...real good

She went into corners
and looked around there
she looked into baskets
and into the air

(There's lots of things here she's not normally
allowed to do.)

then she jumped on the top
and sniffed at a cup

and using her paws

she lifted it up

it dripped  on her foot
it dripped on the floor
it was still a bit wet
from my washing before

Then she dropped it, Oh Dear!
What was going on here?
She was making a mess
that couldn't help less!

But stop! Wait a minute!
What's that on the inside?
it's glittering, it's sparkling,
I looked and I sighed...

Can you see anything
hiding inside?

I couldn't believe it
I wanted to sing
Shadow'd found it
she'd found it
my lost golden ring!

"Oh Shadow Cat, Oh Shadow Cat
you amazingly clever old thing
though I'm sure I'll never know
how you found my lost golden ring

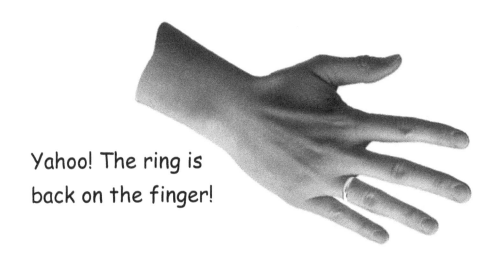

Yahoo! The ring is
back on the finger!

Now I'll be more careful
in future for sure
I'll watch where I put things
I'll keep them secure

Now I'm pleased that this story
has allowed you to meet
this friend of mine
who's light on her feet

a clever detective
and more than just that
the slinkiest, smoochiest,
friendly black cat.

If you want to know how Shadow knew where to look
for the ring you can find out on the next few pages.

# How Did Shadow know where the ring was?
## Well let's see...

First of all she was watching what was going on from her mat

This is the area she could see

And she was watching the washing up (remember it said it in the story)

See, here is the ring...

...and here we're told Shadow is watching

I was just finishing some washing up
Shadow was watching me from her mat

Second when you're hands are soapy rings can fall off and this is how it got in the cup...

Soapy hands so
ring falls off...

...and lands
in the cup...

And remember it was being done in a hurry so it's easy not to notice these things.

So Shadow knew what had happened all along... that's why she didn't bother to go outside (which is where I thought I'd lost it)... she already knew just where it was.

So why did Shadow hunt about, going into corners and baskets, instead of going straight to the right place?

Well she's a cat... and cat's like to find excuses for doing things they're not really allowed to do (like jumping up on kitchen surfaces!) when they know they can get away with it... cat's like to have fun!

So...
if you want to be a Detective you've got to keep your eyes open.
if you're doing things in a hurry you'd better be careful you don't lose something...

... and if you do let's hope you have a good friend to help you find it again.

# Horace the Hippo

# wants to have a bowl

Horace the Hippo was known to be
a world-class batsman
who went in at number three

Here he is batting in a
Test Match at Lords

He knew how to hold a cricket bat
although in his toes it was wobbly
He knew how to whack a cricket ball
although when he ran he was bobbly

But most of all he wanted to bowl
he was sure his deliveries would be deadly
A googly, an off-break, a fast upper cut
a slow one when no one was read-ily

He talked to the captain, he twisted his arm
said letting him bowl wouldn't do any harm
So the Captain he thought for a really long time...
... then said "Oh, go ahead
but please bowl a good line."

So Horace went back to the start of his run
determined to show he could not be out-done
He'd thought up a plan, knew what he'd do
if the ball didn't hit the stumps
he'd use his follow through

So he bowled... ... ... ...

... and the ball it went somewhere...

to be honest with you
the batsman didn't care

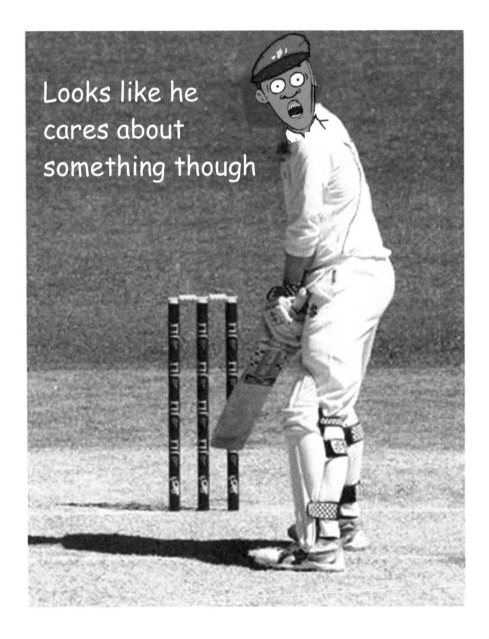

What made him move at the speed of light
was what he was seeing, a terrible sight

Horace had rolled himself up and into a ball
a ball the size of a bus

he was rolling quite fast in a hippo-like way
and travelling all in a rush

The batman just jumped
right out of the way
just like anyone would...
wouldn't you say

And Horace rolled on and mowed down the stumps
while shouting out loudly "How's that!"

The batsman just sighed
and leant on his bat

The bails they were off
that's got to be said
but the umpire looked on
and was scratching his head

He consulted the rules
so he could decide
not wanting to favour
a particular side

Was the batsman all out
or actually still in?
Cos "Hippo-hit-wicket"
was a new one on him

He cleared his throat once
and then said "A-hem!"

"To give me chance
to sort this all out
I'll be needing some time
and a strong cup of tea
and I'll hope to have sussed it
by a quarter to three."

But he never came back
couldn't believe what he saw
so the players shook hands
and they called it a draw

And that's why it's true
all the pundits will say
that you won't see any hippos
playing cricket today

Though I'd like to be clear
to give hippos their due
that it's not the way they bowl
it's their terrifying follow through!

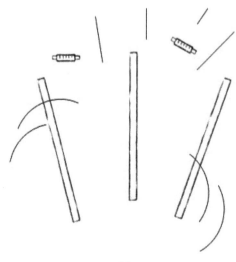

# Even Dinosaurs

# have tricky

# problems...

# Who Knows?

The Tyrannosaurus Rex has got big teeth
but only little arms.
After all these years nobody knows
if they could actually scratch their nose
or if they had to use their toes
or bend their head into a ditch
and rub it roughly on the ground
to get at that annoying itch.

Nobody knows ...

                              ...so you decide!

How did they do it?

# Let me tell you why

# I'm Happy

# to be a Toad !

# I'm not a Frog!

My skin is lumpy and full of warts
not sleek, or smooth or neatly sewed
it looks quite dry not wet or watery
cos I'm not a frog... I'm a toad

Here is my skin
- see all the
beautiful warts?

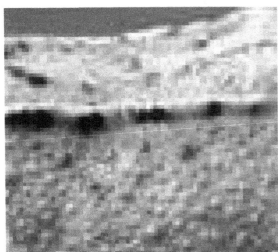

Here is a frog's skin
- far too smooth and
slippery... yeugh!

I like to wander through the grass
to retain my moisture load
I don't dry out, I'm a different class
cos I'm not a frog... I'm a toad

Here's some of the grass
I like to wander through

Can you see me hiding in the grass?

My legs are shorter, not as good at hopping
but better to crawl as they're strong and bowed
and when I'm spotted they're used for stopping
cos I'm not a frog... I'm a toad

Frog's legs -
they're sooo long
and webby!

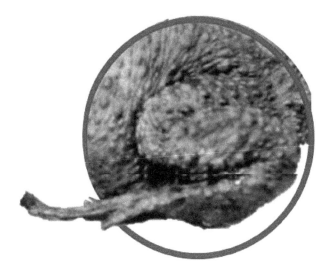

My legs - they're
shorter and stronger.

Wouldn't you like legs
like this?

I might not be lithe nor athletic-looking
I'm dumpy and squat I've been told
But I've got a nose that's good for sniffing
cos I'm not a frog... I'm a toad

Here is a Frog not
too bad looking in
a froggy kind of
way I suppose...

Here is me, aaaah
I am so handsome...

Don't you agree?

My spawn is not clumpy but comes out in rows
in strips and not in a load
it's easy to tell that they're not a frog's
cos I'm not a frog... I'm a toad

Which of
these do you
think is mine?
... and not all
clumpy like a
stinky frog's...

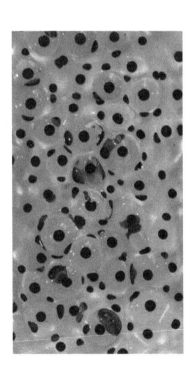
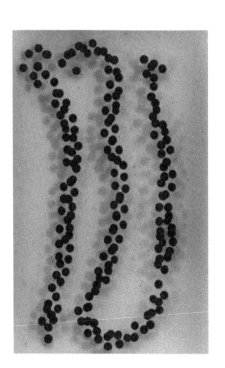

Toad-poles are chunky and almost all black
not slimmer and flecked out with gold
but I don't really mind, I don't care what I lack
cos I'm not a frog... I'm a toad

Here is the tadpole
of a Frog
 - it's just showing off
  if you ask me...

Here is my toad-pole
 - much more attractive...

So toads are much better than frogs I would say
cos we'd give 'em a run for their money all day
though we don't often meet, and we don't often greet
and we'd give 'em a wide berth if we met on the street
I still think this story will never grow old
cos I'm not a frog... I'M A TOAD!!

Here I AM !
And a beautiful thing I am too...

# And Lastly... with my Love

**Abigail**, Abigail, Abigail Ann
She always runs as fast as she can
Over the mountains and right out to sea
But she'll run back home when it's time for her tea

**Benjamin** builds blocks that go up to the sky
One upon one he builds them so high
I'm sure that they'll last him through thunder or rain
But even if not he'll just build them again

**James** is a smiler and a charmer at that
He smiles at his sister and laughs at the cat
And when things go wrong as sometimes they do
He cries then he laughs cos he's tickle-ish too

Lightning Source UK Ltd.
Milton Keynes UK
UKHW051327110821
388628UK00002B/121